DRACULA

Bram Stoker

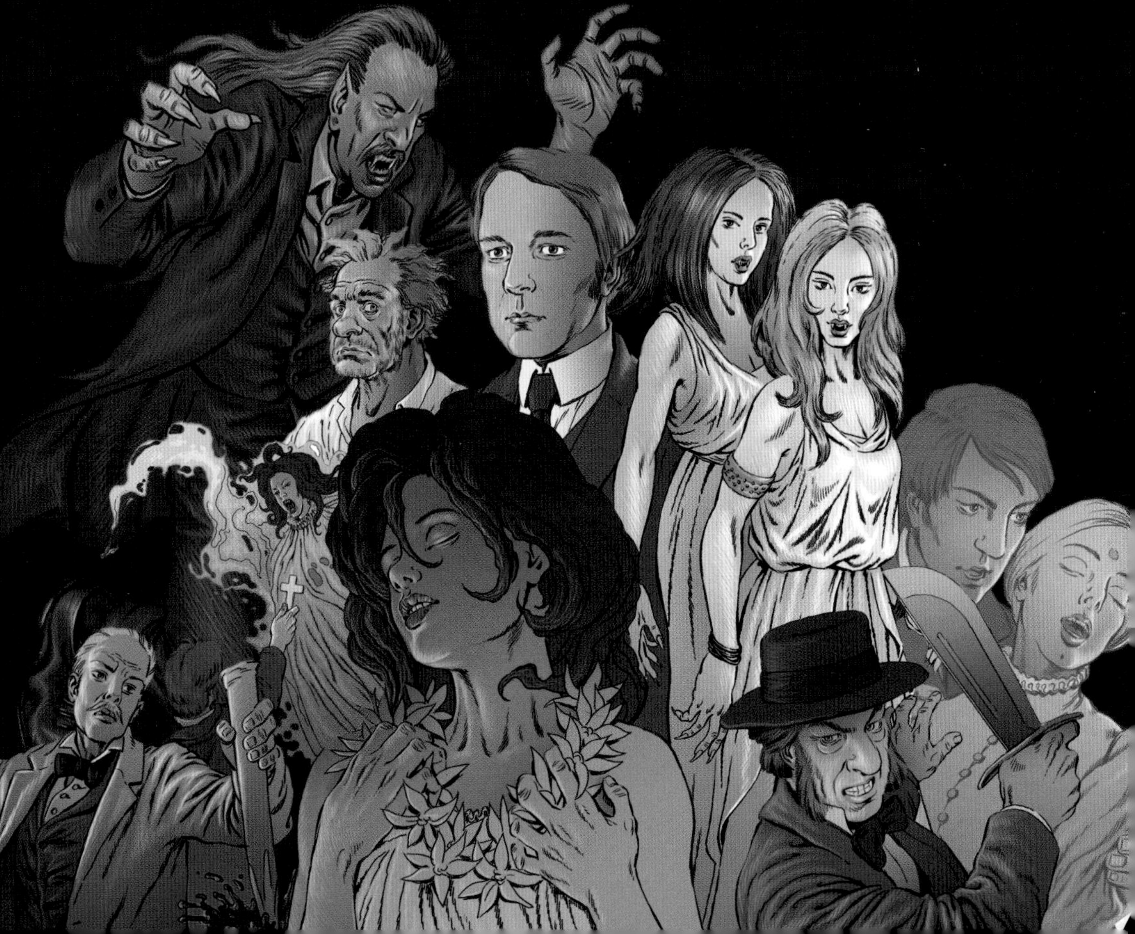

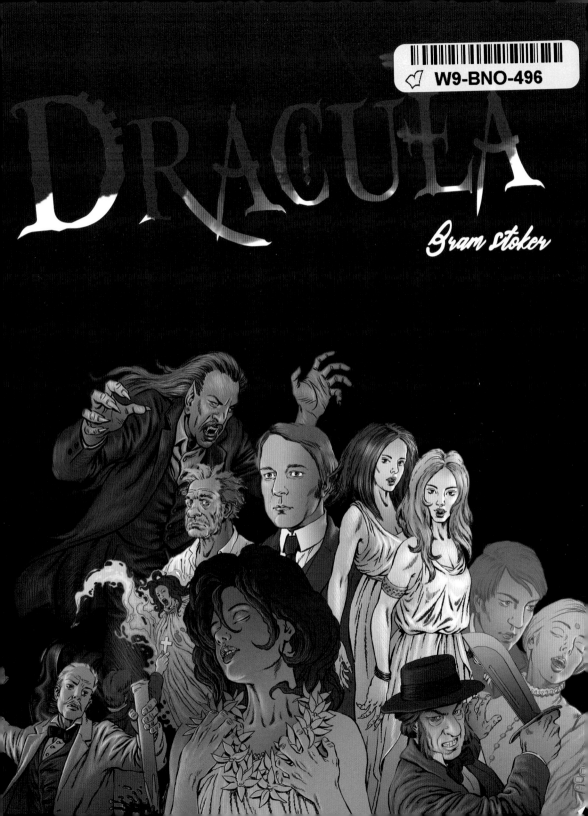

STERLING CHILDREN'S BOOKS
New York

An Imprint of Sterling Publishing Co., Inc.
1166 Avenue of the Americas
New York, NY 10036

STERLING CHILDREN'S BOOKS and the distinctive Sterling Children's Books logo
are registered trademarks of Sterling Publishing Co., Inc.

© 2007 The Salariya Book Company LTD.

ISBN 978-1-4549-3970-2

Distributed in Canada by Sterling Publishing Co., Inc.
c/o Canadian Manda Group, 664 Annette Street
Toronto, Ontario M6S 2C8, Canada

For information about custom editions, special sales, and premium and corporate
purchases, please contact Sterling Special Sales at 800-805-5489
or specialsales@sterlingpublishing.com.

Manufactured in Singapore
Lot #:
2 4 6 8 10 9 7 5 3 1
02/20

sterlingpublishing.com

DRACULA

Bram Stoker

ILLUSTRATED BY
PENKO GELEV

RETOLD BY
FIONA MACDONALD

STERLING CHILDREN'S BOOKS
New York

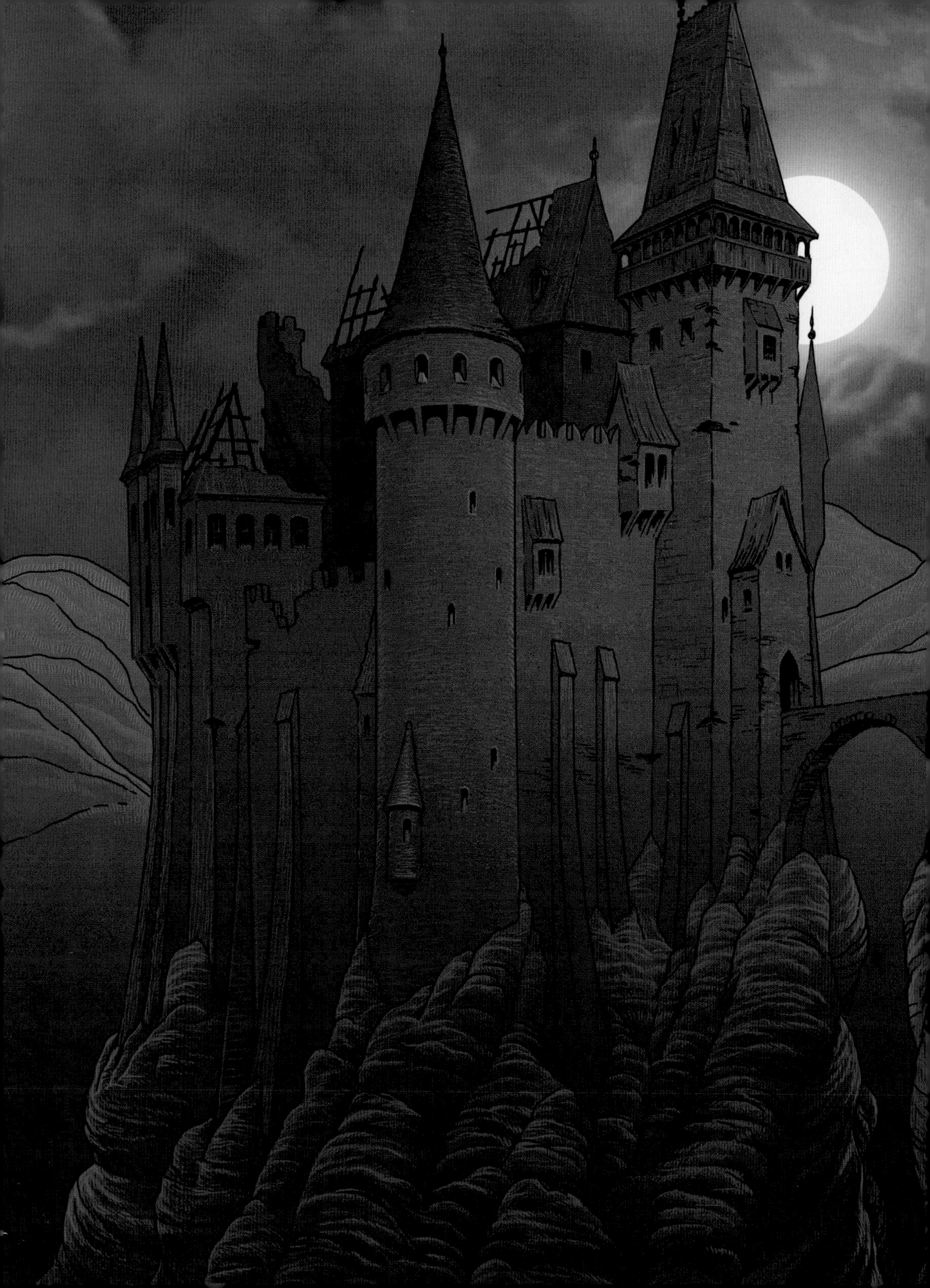

My friend,

Welcome to the Carpathians. I am
anxiously expecting you. Sleep well
tonight. At the Borgo Pass my
carriage will await you and bring you
to me. I trust that your journey from
London has been a happy one, and
that you will enjoy your stay in my
beautiful land.

Sincerely,

Dracula

CHARACTERS

COUNT DRACULA

MINA MURRAY (LATER HARKER)

JONATHAN HARKER

LUCY WESTENRA

LUCY'S MOTHER

PROFESSOR ABRAHAM VAN HELSING

QUINCEY MORRIS

DR. JOHN SEWARD

ARTHUR HOLMWOOD

MR. HAWKINS

R. M. RENFIELD

THE VAMPIRE WOMEN

JONATHAN HARKER IS MAKING HIS FIRST TRIP ABROAD. HE'S A YOUNG ENGLISH LAWYER, ON HIS WAY TO MEET A NEW CLIENT–THE MYSTERIOUS COUNT DRACULA. HE MUST TRAVEL FOR DAYS TO REACH TRANSYLVANIA,[1] DRACULA'S WILD, REMOTE HOMELAND IN THE CARPATHIAN MOUNTAINS.

FAR AWAY FROM ENGLAND, JONATHAN FEELS UNEASY.

JONATHAN REACHES A GLOOMY OLD INN, WHERE HE ASKS FOR NEWS OF DRACULA. THE INNKEEPERS SHUDDER AND INSIST ON GIVING HIM A CRUCIFIX.[2] WHY?

THEY HAND JONATHAN SEALED INSTRUCTIONS SENT BY DRACULA. HE MUST RIDE BY COACH TO THE BORGO PASS[3] –ON ST. GEORGE'S EVE, WHEN THE LOCAL PEOPLE BELIEVE THAT EVIL SPIRITS WANDER. HIS FELLOW TRAVELERS TRY TO WARN JONATHAN OF THE DANGERS, BUT HE DOESN'T UNDERSTAND THEM.

IT'S DARK WHEN THEY REACH THE PASS. A CARRIAGE APPEARS AT BREAKNECK SPEED, DRIVEN BY A TALL MAN WITH GLOWING EYES. JONATHAN CLIMBS ABOARD.

AS THEY DRIVE OFF, WOLVES SNARL AROUND THEM AND EERIE BLUE FLAMES FLICKER IN THE DARKNESS.

AT LAST, THEY REACH A HUGE, HALF-RUINED CASTLE, TOWERING ON THE BRINK OF A PRECIPICE. THE DRIVER VANISHES. THE CASTLE SEEMS DESERTED—BUT FINALLY JONATHAN HEARS FOOTSTEPS. SLOWLY, A LOCKED DOOR OPENS, WITH MUCH CREAKING AND GROANING.

THEY SHAKE HANDS, AND JONATHAN SHIVERS HORRIBLY. DRACULA'S STRONG GRASP IS COLD AND CHILL—IT'S LIKE TOUCHING A DEAD MAN'S FINGERS! DRACULA LEADS THE WAY THROUGH DIM, COBWEBBED HALLS TO A RICHLY FURNISHED CHAMBER.

I TRUST YOU WILL FIND ALL YOU WISH.

—THE CHILDREN OF THE N[...] WHAT MUSIC THEY MAK[...]

WOLVES HOWL OUTSIDE.

JONATHAN IS COLD, TIRED, AND HUNGRY, SO HE ENJOYS THE MEAL THAT HAS BEEN PREPARED FOR HIM. BUT HE'S SURPRISED TO SEE THAT DRACULA DOESN'T EAT OR DRINK ANYTHING.

THE NEXT DAY, JONATHAN SLEEPS LATE. JUST AFTER SUNSET, DRACULA ARRIVES. JONATHAN ASKS ABOUT THE BOOKS ON THE SHELVES. THEY'RE ALL ABOUT ENGLAND— AND THEY'RE IN ENGLISH.

JONATHAN NOTICES DRACULA'S HAIRY PALMS—AND HIS NAILS, SHARP AS CLAWS. NERVOUSLY, HE GOES TO BED. THEY TALKED ALL NIGHT.

DRACULA EXPLAINS WHY

LOVE THE SHADE AND THE SHADOW.

THE HOUSE HE WANTS TO BUY IS CALLED CARFAX. JONATHAN TELLS HIM THAT IT IS A BIG, OLD, DARK HOUSE. DRACULA IS PLEASED: A HOUSE LIKE THIS WILL SUIT HIM.

THAT NIGHT, JONATHAN CAN'T SLEEP. HE GETS UP, AND SHAVES BEFORE SUNRISE. SUDDENLY DRACU APPEARS, LOOMING OUT OF THE DARKNESS. BUT NO REFLECTION IN JONATHAN'S SHAVING MIRROR

JONATHAN'S SO STARTLED THAT HE CUTS HIMSELF WITH HIS RAZOR.

DRACULA BARES HIS POINTED TEETH AND SEEMS TO WANT TO LICK THE BLOOD!

BUT, WHEN HE SEES THE CRUCIFIX GIVEN TO JONATHAN BY THE INNKEEPERS, HE STOPS AT ONCE. ANGRILY, HE THROWS THE MIRROR OUT THE WINDOW.

TAKE CARE! IT IS MORE DANGEROUS THAN YOU THINK IN THIS COUNTRY.

THE CASTLE IS A PRISON . . .

ONCE DRACULA'S GONE, JONATHAN DECIDES HE MUST FIND OUT MORE ABOUT THE CASTLE. BUT HIS DOOR IS LOCKED, AND THERE'S A SHEER CLIFF OUTSIDE THE WINDOW.

. . . AND I AM A PRISONER!

EVERYTHING HIMSELF. WHY IS HE ALL ALONE IN THIS CASTLE?

HIS FAMOUS ANCESTORS. MOST WERE WARRIORS—BRAVE AND PATRIOTIC, BUT UTTERLY RUTHLESS TO THEIR ENEMIES.

WE HAVE A RIGHT TO BE PROUD.

I WILL TAKE NO REFUSAL.

DRACULA WANTS JONATHAN TO STAY A MONTH LONGER IN THE CASTLE.

HE TELLS JONATHAN TO WRITE TO HIS EMPLOYER, MR. HAWKINS, TO SAY THAT HE IS NOT COMING HOME YET. SECRETLY, JONATHAN WRITES TO HIS FIANCÉE, MINA, AS WELL.

THERE ARE BAD DREAMS FOR THOSE WHO SLEEP UNWISELY.

DRACULA WARNS JONATHAN NEVER TO FALL ASLEEP IN THE CASTLE, EXCEPT IN HIS OWN ROOM.

DESPITE HIS FEAR, JONATHAN'S DETERMINED TO EXPLORE. ON A BRIGHT, MOONLIT NIGHT, HE SEARCHES FOR A WINDOW FROM WHICH HE CAN SEE DRACULA'S ROOM.

HE SEES DRACULA, CRAWLING HEADFIRST DOWN THE WALL LIKE SOME HUGE, LOATHSOME[1] LIZARD!

1. LOATHSOME: HORRIBLE, REPULSIVE.

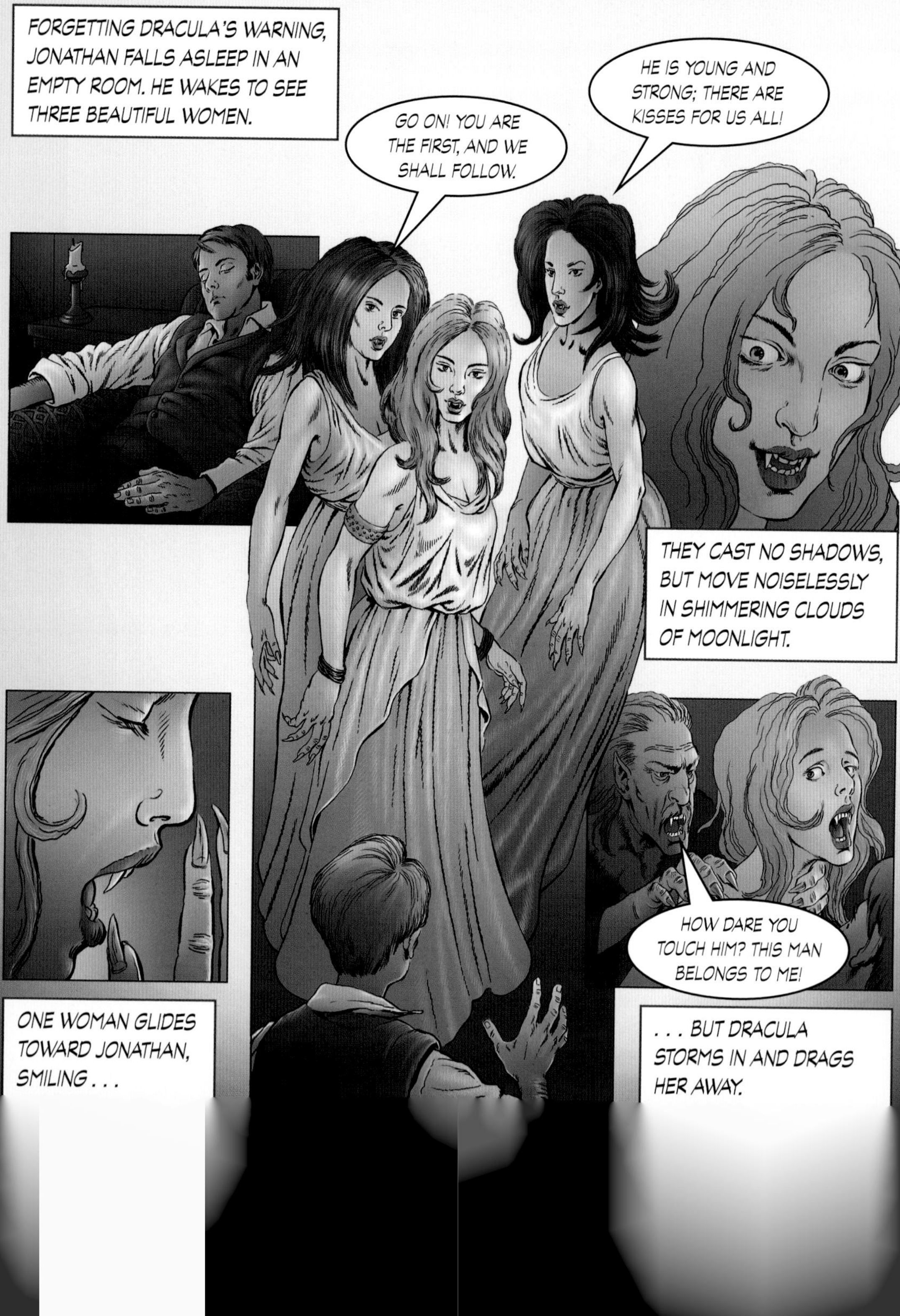
FORGETTING DRACULA'S WARNING, JONATHAN FALLS ASLEEP IN AN EMPTY ROOM. HE WAKES TO SEE THREE BEAUTIFUL WOMEN.
GO ON! YOU ARE THE FIRST, AND WE SHALL FOLLOW.
HE IS YOUNG AND STRONG; THERE ARE KISSES FOR US ALL!
THEY CAST NO SHADOWS, BUT MOVE NOISELESSLY IN SHIMMERING CLOUDS OF MOONLIGHT.
ONE WOMAN GLIDES TOWARD JONATHAN, SMILING . . .
HOW DARE YOU TOUCH HIM? THIS MAN BELONGS TO ME!
. . . BUT DRACULA STORMS IN AND DRAGS HER AWAY.

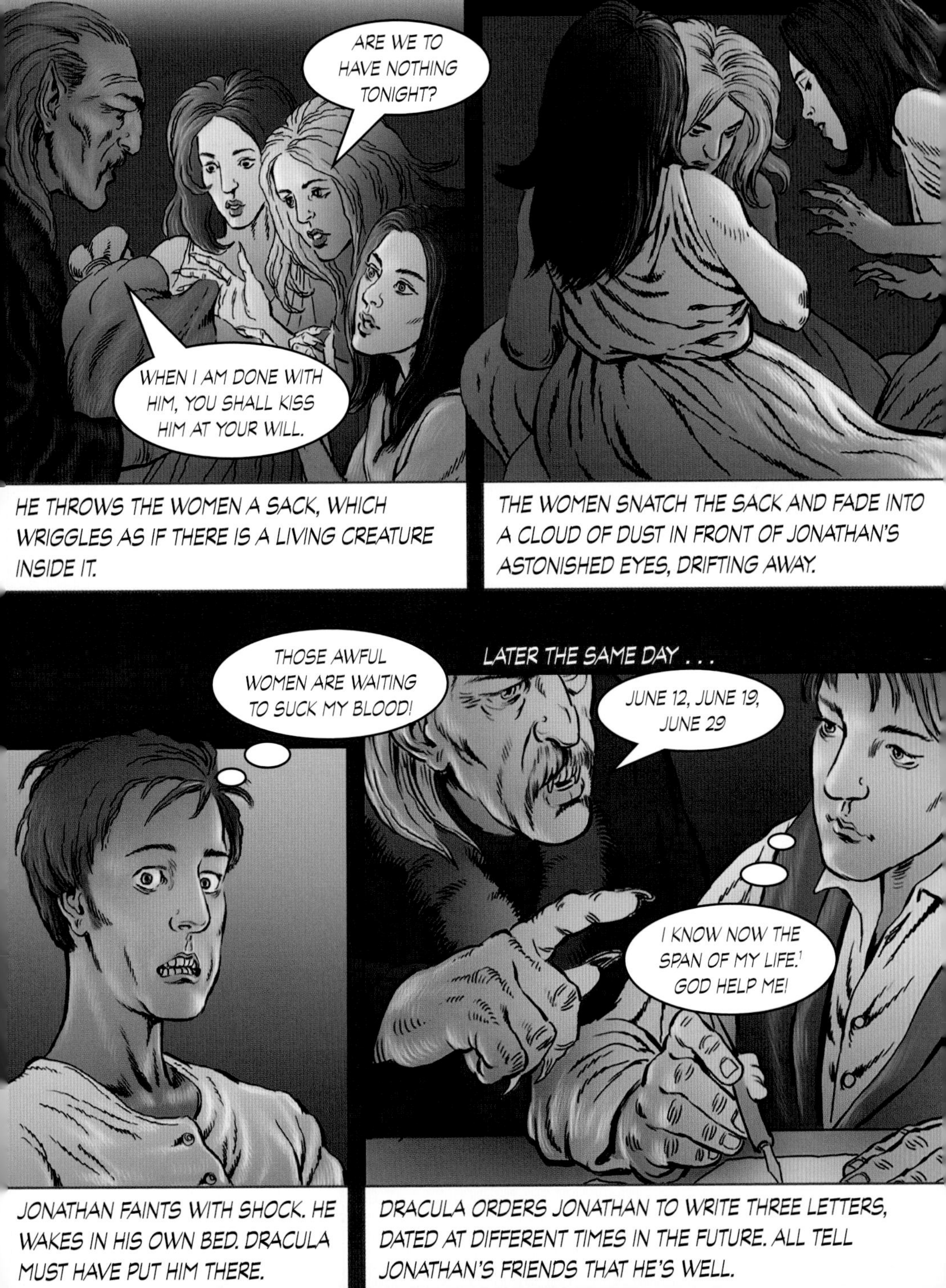
ARE WE TO HAVE NOTHING TONIGHT?
WHEN I AM DONE WITH HIM, YOU SHALL KISS HIM AT YOUR WILL.
HE THROWS THE WOMEN A SACK, WHICH WRIGGLES AS IF THERE IS A LIVING CREATURE INSIDE IT.
THE WOMEN SNATCH THE SACK AND FADE INTO A CLOUD OF DUST IN FRONT OF JONATHAN'S ASTONISHED EYES, DRIFTING AWAY.
THOSE AWFUL WOMEN ARE WAITING TO SUCK MY BLOOD!
JONATHAN FAINTS WITH SHOCK. HE WAKES IN HIS OWN BED. DRACULA MUST HAVE PUT HIM THERE.
LATER THE SAME DAY . . .
JUNE 12, JUNE 19, JUNE 29
I KNOW NOW THE SPAN OF MY LIFE.[1] GOD HELP ME!
DRACULA ORDERS JONATHAN TO WRITE THREE LETTERS, DATED AT DIFFERENT TIMES IN THE FUTURE. ALL TELL JONATHAN'S FRIENDS THAT HE'S WELL.

JONATHAN REALIZES THAT THE LETTERS ARE PART OF DRACULA'S EVIL PLAN: HE WANTS JONATHAN'S FRIENDS TO THINK HE IS SAFE, BUT THEN HE WILL KILL HIM. WHEN SOME ROMA[1] ARRIVE TO WORK AT THE CASTLE, JONATHAN ASKS THEM TO POST HIS SECRET LETTER TO MINA.

AN OUTRAGE!

BUT THEY ARE LOYAL TO DRACULA, AND THEY HAND THE LETTER TO HIM INSTEAD. HE IS FURIOUS AND BURNS THE LETTER.

SOME NEW SCHEME OF VILLAINY . . .

SOON AFTER, JONATHAN FINDS THAT ALL HIS CLOTHES HAVE VANISHED FROM THE WARDROBE.

1. ROMA: TRAVELING PEOPLE.

DRACULA LEAVES THE CASTLE, CARRYING THE SACK THAT HE GAVE TO THE WOMEN. HE IS DISGUISED IN JONATHAN'S CLOTHES.

THE ROMA BRING LARGE WOODEN BOXES.

MONSTER, GIVE ME MY CHILD!

A PEASANT WOMAN HAMMERS AT THE CASTLE GATE, ASKING FOR HER BABY. DRACULA SUMMONS WILD WOLVES, AND THEY KILL HER.

THE ONLY WAY JONATHAN CAN GET OUT OF HIS LOCKED ROOM IS BY CLIMBING OUT THE WINDOW. HE'S TERRIFIED, BUT HE KNOWS HE WILL BE KILLED IF HE DOES NOT ESCAPE.

GOD HELP ME IN MY TASK!

HE FINDS THE WAY TO DRACULA'S ROOM AND CLIMBS IN. IT'S EMPTY, APART FROM HEAPS OF GOLD COINS. ALL OF THEM ARE 300 YEARS OLD OR MORE.

HE MAKES HIS WAY THROUGH A DARK PASSAGE TO THE CHAPEL.

DRACULA'S LYING IN ONE OF THE BOXES, ON A PILE OF EARTH. HIS EYES ARE STARING WIDE, HIS LIPS BLOOD-RED. IS HE DEAD OR ALIVE?

A GRAVEYARD!

NO PULSE, NO BREATH, NO BEATING OF THE HEART . . .

THERE ARE FIFTY WOODEN BOXES, AND THE ROMA WORKMEN HAVE BEEN FILLING THEM WITH EARTH FROM THE CHAPEL FLOOR. WHAT DOES DRACULA NEED THIS FOR? IS IT SOME MYSTERIOUS PART OF HIS PLAN TO MOVE TO ENGLAND?

AWAY FROM THIS CURSED LAND, WHERE THE DEVIL AND HIS CHILDREN STILL WALK!

I MUST RID THE WORLD OF SUCH A MONSTER!

GOODBYE, MINA!

DRACULA MUST NOT BE ALLOWED TO GO TO ENGLAND! JONATHAN RAISES A SHOVEL–BUT DRACULA STIRS, AND JONATHAN LOSES HIS NERVE.

THE WORKMEN ARRIVE TO CARRY THE BOXES AWAY. SWOLLEN WITH BLOOD, DRACULA IS BEING SHIPPED TO ENGLAND.

JONATHAN MAKES ONE LAST ATTEMPT TO ESCAPE BY CLIMBING DOWN THE WALL.

MAY 9, 1897: ENGLAND

SCHOOLTEACHER MINA MURRAY IS WRITING TO HER FRIEND LUCY WESTENRA. MINA IS ENGAGED TO MARRY JONATHAN HARKER, AND TELLS LUCY OF HER HOPES FOR A BUSY, USEFUL FUTURE AS JONATHAN'S WIFE.

LUCY WRITES BACK, FULL OF EXCITEMENT. THREE MEN HAVE ASKED TO MARRY HER, ALL ON THE SAME DAY!

THE FIRST WAS JOHN SEWARD, A HARD-WORKING DOCTOR WHO RUNS A MENTAL HOSPITAL.

THE SECOND WAS QUINCEY MORRIS, A BRAVE TRAVELER FROM THE UNITED STATES.

THE THIRD WAS ARTHUR HOLMWOOD, THE SON OF LORD GODALMING. THE THREE MEN HAVE SWORN TO REMAIN FRIENDS, COME WHAT MAY.

TELL ME ALL THE NEWS WHEN YOU WRITE.

MINA, PRAY FOR MY HAPPINESS!

WON'T YOU JUST HITCH UP ALONGSIDE OF ME?

NO . . . THERE IS SOMEONE ELSE . . .

OH, YES!

OH, MINA, I LOVE HIM!

THIS IS A LOVELY PLACE.

FOOL-TALK!

MINA AND LUCY ARE ON HOLIDAY TOGETHER IN WHITBY. THEY STROLL IN THE PEACEFUL CHURCHYARD, NEXT TO THE ANCIENT RUINS OF WHITBY ABBEY.

THEY MAKE FRIENDS WITH AN ELDERLY FISHERMAN, AND ASK HIM ABOUT THE LOCAL LEGENDS. PEOPLE SAY THAT A GHOST—A WHITE LADY—OFTEN APPEARS THERE.

A HUNDRED YEARS IS TOO MUCH FOR ANY MAN TO EXPECT.

I WISH HE WERE HERE.

THE FISHERMAN SAYS THE GRAVEYARD IS A HOLY PLACE. HE'LL SOON BE LYING THERE HIMSELF.

BUT MINA IS WORRIED ABOUT JONATHAN—SHE HASN'T HEARD FROM HIM FOR WEEKS. AND NOW THERE'S ANOTHER THING TO WORRY ABOUT: LUCY HAS STARTED SLEEPWALKING.

1. WHITBY: A FISHING PORT AND HOLIDAY RESORT IN NORTH YORKSHIRE, ON THE NORTHEAST COAST OF ENGLAND.

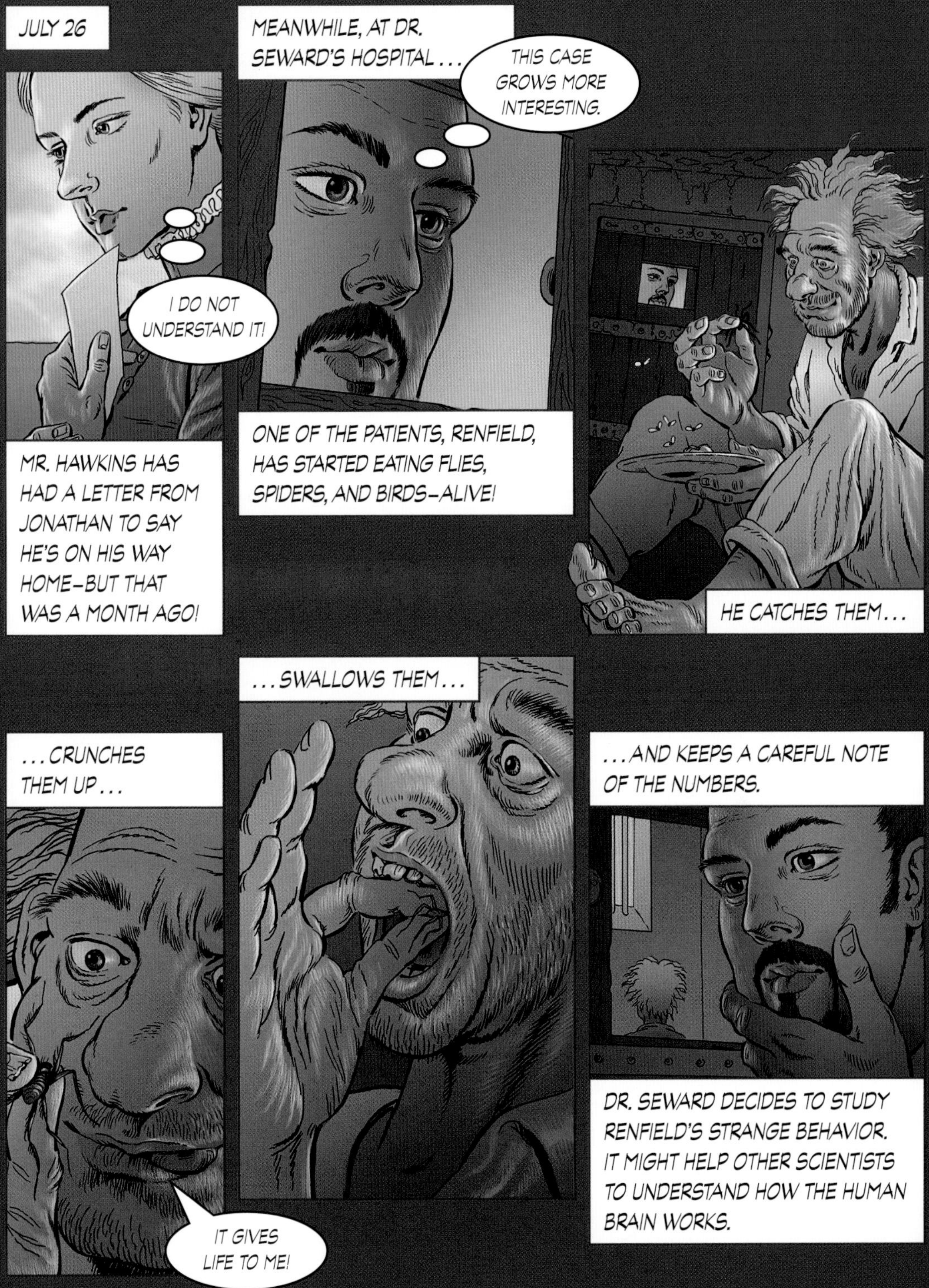
JULY 26
I DO NOT UNDERSTAND IT!
MR. HAWKINS HAS HAD A LETTER FROM JONATHAN TO SAY HE'S ON HIS WAY HOME–BUT THAT WAS A MONTH AGO!
MEANWHILE, AT DR. SEWARD'S HOSPITAL . . .
THIS CASE GROWS MORE INTERESTING.
ONE OF THE PATIENTS, RENFIELD, HAS STARTED EATING FLIES, SPIDERS, AND BIRDS–ALIVE!
HE CATCHES THEM . . .
. . . CRUNCHES THEM UP . . .
IT GIVES LIFE TO ME!
. . . SWALLOWS THEM . . .
. . . AND KEEPS A CAREFUL NOTE OF THE NUMBERS.
DR. SEWARD DECIDES TO STUDY RENFIELD'S STRANGE BEHAVIOR. IT MIGHT HELP OTHER SCIENTISTS TO UNDERSTAND HOW THE HUMAN BRAIN WORKS.

AUGUST 8, 1897: WHITBY IS BLASTED BY A TERRIBLE STORM.

A RUSSIAN SAILING SHIP RUNS AGROUND. THERE'S NO SIGN OF LIFE ON BOARD, EXCEPT FOR A HUGE DOG THAT LEAPS ASHORE AND RUNS AWAY.

DEAD!

ONCE THE STORM HAS DIED DOWN, WHITBY SAILORS EXPLORE THE WRECK. THEY FIND THE CAPTAIN AT THE WHEEL, CLUTCHING THE WHEEL.

THE TALE OF THE SHIP'S LOG:

THERE'S SOMETHING ABOARD!

THERE'S NOT MUCH CARGO—JUST BIG BOXES OF EARTH. BUT THE SHIP'S LOG-BOOK TELLS AN EXTRAORDINARY STORY.

AFTER SAILING FROM VARNA,[1] THE CREW COMPLAINED THAT AN EVIL PRESENCE WAS HAUNTING THEM.

THE WEATHER WAS AWFUL, AND SAILORS MYSTERIOUSLY VANISHED IN THE NIGHT. ONE NIGHT, ONE OF THE SAILORS SAW A GHOSTLY FIGURE.

EMPTY AS THE AIR!

THE SEA WILL SAVE ME FROM HIM!

IT IS HERE! I KNOW IT, NOW!

THE MATE[2] ATTACKED IT WITH HIS KNIFE—BUT HIS HAND PASSED STRAIGHT THROUGH! MAD WITH FEAR, THE MATE JUMPED OVERBOARD.

1. VARNA: A RUSSIAN PORT ON THE BLACK SEA.
2. MATE: SECOND IN COMMAND.

BY NOW, ONLY THE CAPTAIN WAS LEFT ALIVE. HE SAID HIS PRAYERS, TIED HIS HANDS TO THE WHEEL, AND DIED IN THE STORM.

THE OLD FISHERMAN HAS BEEN FOUND DEAD IN WHITBY CHURCHYARD, HIS NECK BROKEN.

EVERYONE'S SHOCKED TO SEE THE LOOK OF HORROR ON HIS FACE, AS IF HE HAD SEEN DEATH.

POOR DEAR OLD MAN!

LUCY! LUCY!

ITS FACE IS WHITE, ITS EYES GLOW RED.

AUGUST 11, 1897

MINA WAKES IN THE NIGHT TO FIND LUCY MISSING. SLEEPWALKING AGAIN! MINA HURRIES AFTER HER. SHE FINDS HER IN THE CHURCHYARD, STRETCHED OUT ON A TOMB—WITH A GHOSTLY SHAPE BENDING OVER HER.

WHEN MINA REACHES LUCY, THE CREATURE HAS GONE. LUCY IS CLUTCHING HER THROAT. MINA PUTS HER SHAWL AROUND LUCY'S SHOULDERS.

THE NEXT DAY, LUCY SAYS SHE'S FINE, BUT MINA SEES TWO LITTLE WOUNDS ON HER NECK. PERHAPS MINA PRICKED HER ACCIDENTALLY WITH THE PIN OF HER SHAWL?

LATER ON, LUCY FEELS ANXIOUS AND RESTLESS AT NIGHT. SHE SLEEPWALKS AND GAZES OUT OF THE WINDOW, TRYING TO GET OUT. MINA LOOKS AFTER HER CAREFULLY.

I SHALL LOCK THE DOOR.

ONE NIGHT, A HUGE BLACK BAT FLUTTERS OUTSIDE THEIR ROOM. IT SEEMS TO BE CALLING TO LUCY. SHE GETS OUT OF BED AND TRIES TO FOLLOW IT, STILL SLEEPING.

SHE IS FRETTING ABOUT SOMETHING. I WISH I COULD FIND OUT WHAT IT IS.

HIS RED EYES AGAIN! THEY ARE JUST THE SAME.

THE NEXT DAY, IN THE CHURCHYARD, LUCY SPIES A TALL, STRANGE-LOOKING FIGURE. SHE STARTLES MINA—AND HERSELF—BY SEEMING TO RECOGNIZE HIM.

ALL THIS TIME, LUCY HAS BEEN GROWING THIN AND PALE, AND THE WOUNDS ON HER NECK DO NOT SEEM TO BE HEALING.

JOY, JOY, JOY!

NEWS AT LAST! MINA GETS A LETTER FROM A HOSPITAL IN HUNGARY. JONATHAN HAS ESCAPED ALIVE FROM DRACULA'S CASTLE…

…BUT THE DREADFUL THINGS HE SAW THERE GAVE HIM A DANGEROUS BRAIN FEVER. HE'S WEAK BUT GETTING BETTER. MINA HURRIES TO HIM.

MINA!

SO THIN AND PALE AND WEAK . . .

I WILL!

I WILL!

THEY GET MARRIED STRAIGHT AWAY, WITHOUT WAITING UNTIL JONATHAN IS WELL ENOUGH TO TRAVEL.

MEANWHILE, BACK IN WHITBY:

I AM FULL OF LIFE!

LUCY'S FIANCÉE ARTHUR ARRIVES TO LOOK AFTER HER. SHE FEELS MUCH BETTER NOW: SHE STOPS SLEEPWALKING AND LOOKS PRETTIER THAN EVER.

AT DR. SEWARD'S HOSPITAL:

THE PATIENT RENFIELD IS BEHAVING VERY STRANGELY. HE'S CRAWLING ON ALL FOURS, SNIFFING LIKE A DOG. HE KEEPS RUNNING AWAY TO CARFAX, A HOUSE NEARBY WHICH HAS JUST BEEN BOUGHT BY A FOREIGN GENTLEMAN.

THE MASTER IS AT HAND.[1]

1. AT HAND: NEARLY HERE.

I HAVE WORSHIPPED YOU! NOW YOU ARE NEAR!

I SHALL BE PATIENT, MASTER. IT IS COMING!

RENFIELD FIGHTS THE NURSES, BUT CALMS DOWN SUDDENLY WHEN HE SEES A HUGE BAT FLYING ACROSS THE MOON.

HE GOES QUIETLY BACK TO HIS ROOM, CATCHING FLIES AS BEFORE.

BUT HE STILL HAS SUDDEN RAGES. DURING ONE OF THESE, HE ATTACKS DR. SEWARD WITH A SHARP KNIFE.

THE BLOOD IS THE LIFE.

HE THEN TRIES TO LICK UP THE DROPS OF BLOOD FROM THE FLOOR OF HIS CELL.

ESCAPING AGAIN TO CARFAX, HE FIGHTS WITH CARRIERS BRINGING HEAVY BOXES OF EARTH—FROM THE WRECKED RUSSIAN SHIP AT WHITBY!

AUGUST 24, 1897

I FEEL SO WEAK.

SHE LOOKS AWFUL.

LUCY, NOW BACK HOME WITH HER MOTHER, IS ILL AGAIN. HER NECK HURTS, AND SHE HAS NIGHTMARES.

SHE'S SLEEPWALKING AGAIN, AND KEEPS SEEING STRANGE THINGS OUTSIDE HER WINDOW. ARTHUR'S ALARMED AND CALLS FOR HIS GOOD FRIEND DR. JOHN SEWARD.

SEWARD, PUZZLED, DECIDES TO ASK HIS WISE OLD TUTOR, PROFESSOR ABRAHAM VAN HELSING. THE PROFESSOR HURRIES TO HELP LUCY, ALL THE WAY FROM AMSTERDAM.

THIS IS DREADFUL. THERE IS NO TIME TO BE LOST.

YOU HAVE SAVED HER LIFE.

I WOULD DIE FOR HER!

VAN HELSING SAYS LUCY'S ILLNESS IS WORRYING BUT NOT DANGEROUS. BUT THAT NIGHT SHE GETS WORSE. SHE HAS LOST BLOOD AND NEEDS A TRANSFUSION.[1] ARTHUR OFFERS TO GIVE HIS BLOOD FOR LUCY, AND SHE IS SAVED–FOR NOW.

1. TRANSFUSION: BLOOD TRANSFUSION WAS DANGEROUS IN THE 19TH CENTURY, BECAUSE SCIENTISTS HAD NOT YET DISCOVERED THAT DIFFERENT BLOOD GROUPS MUST NOT BE MIXED. IT WAS USED ONLY IN DIRE EMERGENCIES.

...AND BY MORNING, SHE IS WORSE THAN EVER. VAN HELSING RETURNS AND GIVES HER SOME OF SEWARD'S BLOOD. AGAIN, LUCY RECOVERS.

VAN HELSING IS WORRIED ABOUT LUCY'S NECK WOUNDS. HE MUST GO HOME TO CONSULT HIS TEXTBOOKS.

SEWARD GUARDS LUCY ALL THROUGH THE NIGHT. SHE SLEEPS PEACEFULLY. BUT THE NEXT NIGHT, LUCY SLEEPS ALONE...

THESE ARE MEDICINES.

THE ROOM IS AWFULLY STUFFY!

VAN HELSING SHUTS LUCY'S WINDOW, GIVES HER GARLIC FLOWERS TO WEAR, AND HANGS GARLIC AT THE WINDOW. FOR A WHILE, LUCY FEELS BETTER.

BUT NO ONE EXPLAINS TO LUCY'S MOTHER WHAT THE GARLIC IS FOR! SHE TAKES IT AWAY AND OPENS THE WINDOW, THINKING THAT FRESH AIR WILL BE GOOD FOR LUCY...

... AND BY MORNING SHE IS CLOSE TO DEATH.

THE POWERS OF THE DEVILS ARE AGAINST US!

YET ANOTHER TRANSFUSION IS NEEDED, THIS TIME FROM VAN HELSING HIMSELF.

CRASH!

A FEW NIGHTS LATER, AS LUCY AND HER MOTHER LIE AWAKE, THEY HEAR HOWLING ALL AROUND. SUDDENLY THE BEDROOM WINDOW SHATTERS. IN THE OPENING, THE TWO WOMEN SEE THE HEAD OF A GREAT GRAY WOLF.

TERRIFIED, LUCY'S MOTHER CLUTCHES AT THE GARLIC FLOWERS, TEARING THEM FROM LUCY'S NECK. SHE FALLS BACK ONTO THE BED. LUCY REALIZES THAT HER MOTHER HAS DIED OF FRIGHT, AND COLLAPSES BESIDE HER.

ALONE WITH THE DEAD! GOD HELP ME!

LUCY CANNOT MOVE, AS THOUGH SHE IS UNDER A SPELL. THE WOLF HAS GONE, AND THE AIR IS FILLED WITH A SHIMMERING, MOONLIT DUST THAT POURS IN THROUGH THE BROKEN WINDOW.

> IT IS NOT YET TOO LATE. QUICK! QUICK!

> A BRAVE MAN'S BLOOD IS THE BEST THING ON EARTH!

SEPTEMBER 18, 1897

THE NEXT MORNING, SEWARD AND VAN HELSING FIGHT TO SAVE LUCY'S LIFE. THIS TIME QUINCEY MORRIS OFFERS HIS BLOOD. BUT WHERE HAS ALL THE TRANSFUSED BLOOD GONE? WHO, OR WHAT, IS TAKING IT FROM HER?

DR. SEWARD WATCHES OVER LUCY THAT NIGHT. IT SEEMS TO HIM THAT HER TEETH LOOK SHARPER THAN USUAL. ONCE AGAIN, A HUGE BAT FLAPS OUTSIDE.

IN HER SLEEP, LUCY PUSHES THE GARLIC FLOWERS AWAY.

BY MORNING, HER NECK WOUNDS HAVE VANISHED. VAN HELSING SUMMONS ARTHUR AT ONCE.

LUCY WAKES AND ASKS ARTHUR FOR A FAREWELL KISS. SHE LOOKS SO LOVELY! HE'S HEARTBROKEN.

SHE IS DYING. IT WILL NOT BE LONG NOW.

OH, MY LOVE!

BUT VAN HELSING PUSHES THEM APART. LUCY IS FURIOUS! A CRUEL LOOK COMES INTO HER EYES; SHE SNARLS LIKE AN ANIMAL.

NOT FOR YOUR LIFE!

GRRRR!

BUT FINALLY LUCY'S OLD, SWEET SELF RETURNS, AND SHE DIES PEACEFULLY. VAN HELSING PLACES A CRUCIFIX ON LUCY'S MOUTH...

. . . BUT IN THE MORNING HE DISCOVERS THAT THE HOUSEMAID HAS STOLEN IT. HE SAYS THEY MUST NOW REMOVE LUCY'S HEAD AND HEART. SEWARD IS HORRIFIED!

MINA AND JONATHAN HARKER HAVE COME BACK TO ENGLAND AND ARE BUSY WORKING TOGETHER. MR. HAWKINS HAS DIED AND LEFT THEM HIS HOUSE AND HIS LAW BUSINESS. JONATHAN IS NOT YET FULLY RECOVERED.

I BELIEVE IT IS THE COUNT, BUT HE HAS GROWN YOUNG!

ONE DAY, ON A VISIT TO LONDON, MINA SEES JONATHAN STARING AT A TALL MAN WITH RED LIPS AND WHITE, POINTED TEETH. JONATHAN SEEMS TO RECOGNIZE HIM.

JONATHAN IS SHOCKED AND HAS TO REST. MINA KNOWS THAT JONATHAN KEPT A SECRET DIARY IN TRANSYLVANIA, AND SHE NOW DECIDES THAT SHE MUST READ IT. ONCE SHE KNOWS WHAT HE'S SUFFERED, SHE MAY BE ABLE TO HELP.

BACK HOME, THEY HEAR THE SAD NEWS THAT LUCY AND HER MOTHER HAVE DIED. WITH A SORROWFUL HEART, MINA STARTS TO READ JONATHAN'S DIARY. IT'S TERRIFYING!

1. EXETER: THE CITY IN THE WEST OF ENGLAND WHERE JONATHAN WORKS AS A LAWYER.

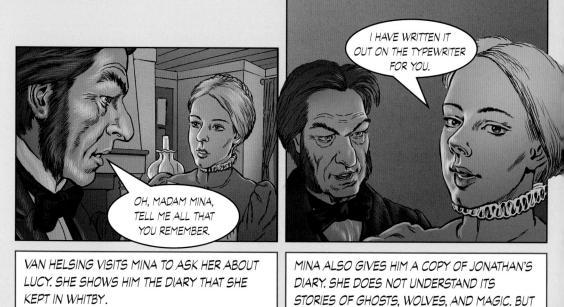

VAN HELSING VISITS MINA TO ASK HER ABOUT LUCY. SHE SHOWS HIM THE DIARY THAT SHE KEPT IN WHITBY.

MINA ALSO GIVES HIM A COPY OF JONATHAN'S DIARY. SHE DOES NOT UNDERSTAND ITS STORIES OF GHOSTS, WOLVES, AND MAGIC. BUT VAN HELSING TELLS HER THAT JONATHAN ISN'T MAD—ALL HE HAS WRITTEN IS TRUE!

THE VISIT ENDS, AND JONATHAN TAKES VAN HELSING TO THE RAILWAY STATION. HE BUYS NEWSPAPERS FOR THE JOURNEY.

THE HEADLINES ARE SHOCKING: CHILDREN IN LONDON HAVE BEEN FOUND HALF-DEAD, WITH BITES ON THEIR NECKS!

MY GOD! SO SOON! SO SOON!

VAN HELSING VISITS DR. SEWARD.

IN GOD'S NAME, PROFESSOR, WHAT DO YOU MEAN?

VAN HELSING SAYS THAT LUCY HAS BEEN KILLED BY A BLOOD-SUCKING CREATURE. NOW ANOTHER SUCH MONSTER IS ON THE PROWL...

THOSE HOLES IN THE CHILDREN'S THROATS WERE MADE BY MISS LUCY!

...AND HE THINKS IT IS LUCY! SEWARD CANNOT BELIEVE THIS, BUT VAN HELSING SAYS HE WILL PROVE IT.

THE BLOOFER[1] LADY...

TOGETHER THEY VISIT THE HOSPITAL. THE CHILDREN HAVE BITE WOUNDS ON THEIR NECKS, LIKE LUCY'S.

1. BLOOFER: A CHILDISH WAY OF SAYING "BEAUTIFUL."

THAT NIGHT, THEY GO TO THE LONDON CHURCHYARD WHERE LUCY IS BURIED.

THEY FIND HER TOMB—BUT IT'S EMPTY! THIS DOES NOT SURPRISE VAN HELSING, BUT SEWARD IS HORRIFIED.

WHAT ARE YOU GOING TO DO?

THEY GO OUTSIDE AND SEE A SMALL CHILD IN THE CHURCHYARD. A GHOSTLY FIGURE IS BENDING OVER IT!

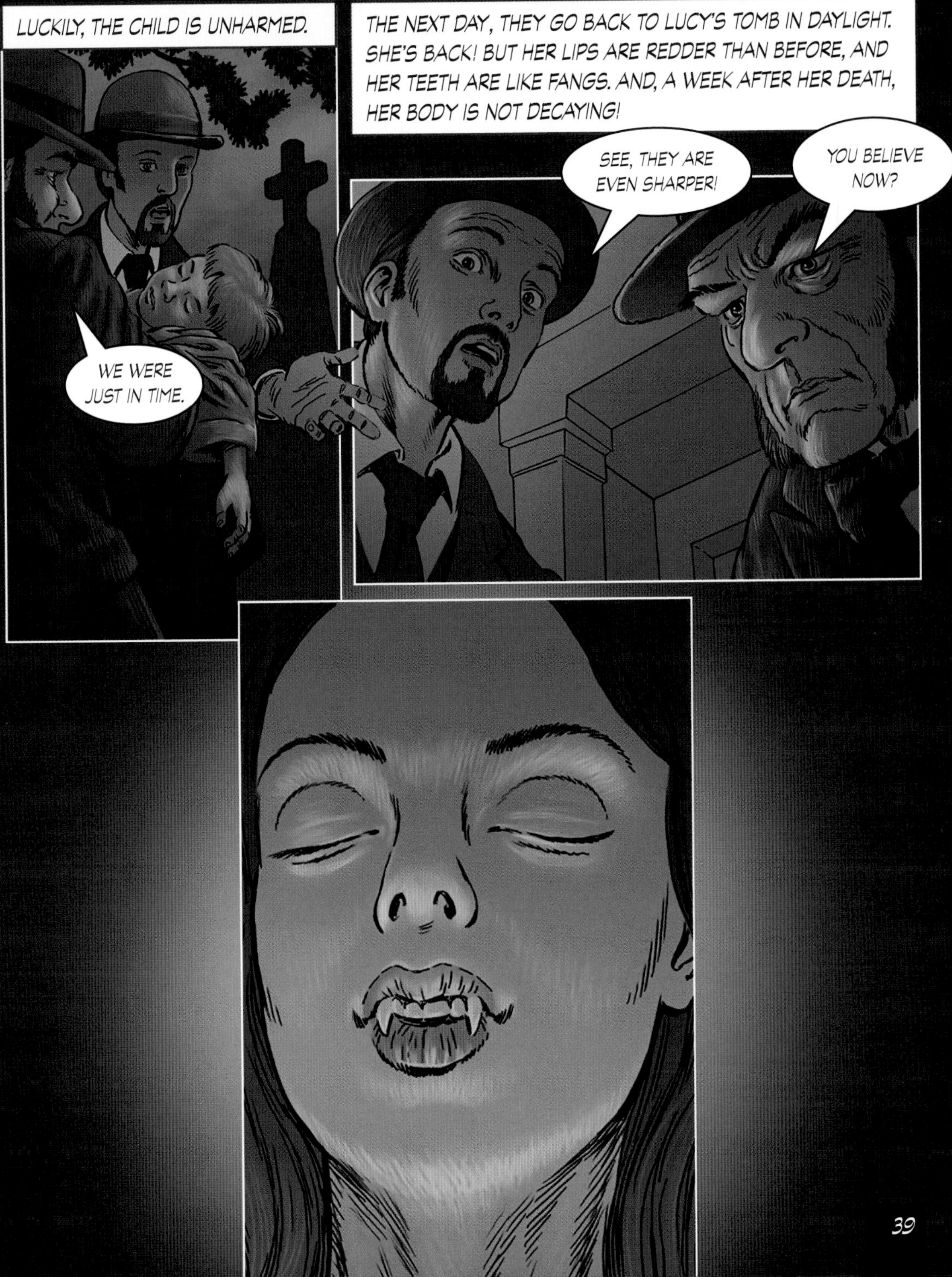
LUCKILY, THE CHILD IS UNHARMED.
WE WERE JUST IN TIME.
THE NEXT DAY, THEY GO BACK TO LUCY'S TOMB IN DAYLIGHT. SHE'S BACK! BUT HER LIPS ARE REDDER THAN BEFORE, AND HER TEETH ARE LIKE FANGS. AND, A WEEK AFTER HER DEATH, HER BODY IS NOT DECAYING!
SEE, THEY ARE EVEN SHARPER!
YOU BELIEVE NOW?

VAN HELSING EXPLAINS:

SHE IS UNDEAD!

LUCY HAS BEEN BITTEN BY A VAMPIRE—A MONSTER THAT FEEDS ON THE BLOOD OF LIVING PEOPLE. SHE HAS BECOME A VAMPIRE, TOO.

THE UNDEAD ARE DESPERATE.

LIKE THE GHOSTLY WOMEN IN DRACULA'S CASTLE, SHE IS NOW A HELLISH, BLOOD-SUCKING CREATURE.

IS THIS ALL A NIGHTMARE?

TO GIVE LUCY PEACE, AND SAVE HER SOUL, SHE MUST BE KILLED ONCE AGAIN.

THIS IS A MYSTERY...

VAN HELSING SEALS THE DOOR OF THE TOMB WITH A PASTE MADE FROM COMMUNION WAFER.[1]

THEY WAIT, UNTIL A GHOSTLY
FIGURE APPEARS IN THE DISTANCE.
IT'S LUCY.

SHHH!

COME TO ME, ARTHUR.
LEAVE THESE OTHERS
AND COME TO ME.

WILD AND BLOODSTAINED, LUCY
GLIDES TOWARD ARTHUR. HER
VOICE IS DEVILISHLY SWEET.

BUT VAN HELSING'S CRUCIFIX
HALTS HER. SHE SPITS AND
GROWLS VICIOUSLY.

LUCY BACKS AWAY WHILE
VAN HELSING REMOVES SOME
OF THE WAFER. SHE SLIDES
THROUGH THE TINY CRACK . . .

...AND RETURNS TO HER COFFIN.

I SHALL NOT FALTER![1]

NOW ARTHUR MUST ACT. HE HAMMERS A WOODEN STAKE THROUGH VAMPIRE LUCY'S HEART. SHE WRITHES AND SCREAMS, THEN GROWS CALM AND STILL. LUCY IS NO LONGER A MONSTER—NOW HER SOUL CAN GO TO HEAVEN.

AAAARGGH!

ARTHUR KISSES LUCY ONE LAST
TIME. NOW IT'S FAREWELL, FOREVER.

THERE'S ONE MORE DREADFUL DUTY. VAN
HELSING CUTS OFF LUCY'S HEAD, THEN FILLS
HER MOUTH WITH GARLIC AND SEALS THE TOMB.

ONE STEP OF
OUR WORK IS DONE,
BUT THERE REMAINS A
GREATER TASK . . .

LUCY'S SOUL IS SAVED, BUT DRACULA—THE
VAMPIRE WHO ATTACKED HER—IS STILL FREE,
AND NOW HE'S SEEKING VICTIMS IN ENGLAND.
HE MUST BE DESTROYED, SOMEHOW!

MINA VISITS DR. SEWARD AT HIS HOSPITAL.

THAT IS A WONDERFUL MACHINE!

SHE OFFERS TO TYPE OUT THE NOTES DR. SEWARD HAS BEEN KEEPING. THESE NOTES WILL HELP THEM ALL TO UNDERSTAND THE TERRIBLE EVENTS MORE CLEARLY.

WE HAVE PUT ALL THE PAPERS IN ORDER.

JONATHAN AND MINA ARE TO STAY WITH DR. SEWARD AT THE HOSPITAL. THEY MAKE A LIST OF EVERYTHING THEY KNOW SO FAR ABOUT DRACULA.

LET ME BE A SISTER TO YOU IN YOUR TROUBLE.

ARTHUR ARRIVES. HE'S OVERCOME WITH GRIEF FOR HIS LUCY. MINA TRIES TO COMFORT HIM.

I WISH I COULD COMFORT ALL WHO SUFFER.

LUCY'S DEATH HAS ALSO MADE QUINCEY MORRIS VERY UNHAPPY. HE SAYS THEY MUST WORK TOGETHER TO TRACK DOWN HER KILLER.

FOR THE BLOOD IS THE LIFE...

SEWARD TAKES MINA TO VISIT HIS STRANGE PATIENT, RENFIELD. WITH MINA, RENFIELD IS POLITE AND DESCRIBES HIS ODD THOUGHTS AND FEELINGS CALMLY.

FOR THE FIRST TIME, ALL THE FRIENDS MEET TOGETHER. VAN HELSING EXPLAINS WHAT VAMPIRES ARE. THEY HAVE NO SHADOW OR REFLECTION, AND THEY SLEEP IN GRAVEYARD DIRT. THEY CAN CHANGE SHAPE—INTO WOLVES OR BATS, FOR EXAMPLE—AND THEY GROW YOUNG AGAIN AFTER DRINKING FRESH BLOOD.

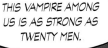

THIS VAMPIRE AMONG US IS AS STRONG AS TWENTY MEN.

IT IS A TERRIBLE TASK THAT WE UNDERTAKE, FOR IF WE FAIL HE WILL SURELY WIN.

WE ARE DETERMINED TO DESTROY THIS MONSTER.

GARLIC AND CRUCIFIXES WILL STOP A VAMPIRE. VAMPIRES CAN'T KILL IN DAYLIGHT, CROSS RUNNING WATER, OR ENTER A HOUSE UNINVITED. A STAKE THROUGH THE HEART WILL KILL THEM; CUTTING OFF THE HEAD BRINGS THEM PEACE.

DRACULA HAS BOUGHT THE HOUSE AT CARFAX, CLOSE TO THE HOSPITAL.

BANG!

EEEEK!

HE'S HAD 50 BOXES OF GRAVEYARD DIRT BROUGHT THERE FROM HIS CASTLE CHAPEL—BY THE HAUNTED SHIP WRECKED AT WHITBY.

AS SOON AS DRACULA'S FULL OF BLOOD, HE'LL SLEEP IN ONE OF THOSE BOXES UNTIL HE'S READY TO ATTACK AGAIN.

SORRY!

QUINCEY HAD SEEN A GIANT BAT OUTSIDE AND TRIED TO SHOOT IT!

AT THE SAME TIME:

LET ME OUT OF THIS! WOE IS ME!

HEAR ME! HEAR ME! LET ME GO!

RENFIELD IS BEGGING THE NURSES TO SET HIM FREE. SEWARD IS CALLED TO SEE HIM. RENFIELD TALKS SENSIBLY AT FIRST, THEN BECOMES FRANTIC.

HE SAYS HE HAS AN IMPORTANT REASON FOR WANTING TO BE LET OUT, BUT HE WILL NOT SAY WHAT IT IS. IS IT SOMETHING TO DO WITH "THE MASTER," PERHAPS?

OCTOBER 1, 1897

IN MANUS TUAS, DOMINE! [1]

MY FRIENDS, WE ARE GOING INTO TERRIBLE DANGER!

THE MEN ARM THEMSELVES WITH KNIVES, GUNS, WAFERS, CRUCIFIXES, AND GARLIC AND GO TO THE CHAPEL AT CARFAX TO HUNT FOR DRACULA'S BOXES, BUT THEY CAN FIND ONLY 29. WHAT HAS DRACULA DONE WITH THE OTHERS?

ARTHUR WHISTLES FOR HIS DOGS. THEY ARE AFRAID AT FIRST, BUT AT LAST THEY CHASE THE RATS AWAY.

THEY THINK THEY SEE A TALL FIGURE IN THE DOORWAY—THEN HUNDREDS OF RATS SQUIRM ALL OVER THE CHAPEL FLOOR.

IT WAS ONLY THE SHADOWS.

GRRR!

1. IN MANUS TUAS, DOMINE: WE PUT OURSELVES IN YOUR HANDS, LORD (LATIN).

MEANWHILE...

I FEEL STRANGELY SAD AND LOW-SPIRITED.

ALL DAY, MINA HAS BEEN LOOKING VERY TIRED AND PALE.

SHE CAN'T FORGET SOMETHING THAT HAPPENED THE PREVIOUS NIGHT. SHE COULDN'T SLEEP, SO SHE LOOKED OUT THE WINDOW.

A THICK MIST CAME CREEPING INTO THE BEDROOM—AND TURNED INTO A GHOSTLY FIGURE WITH GLOWING RED EYES! WAS IT A DREAM?

OCTOBER 2, 1897

MEANWHILE...

HIS MOOD CHANGES SO QUICKLY.

LATER THE SAME NIGHT:

UUURGH!

JONATHAN DISCOVERS THAT DRACULA HAS BOUGHT A HOUSE IN LONDON.

RENFIELD SEEMS TO WANT TO TALK ABOUT "SOULS" AND "BLOOD." SEWARD JUST CAN'T UNDERSTAND HIM.

RENFIELD HAS BEEN INJURED FIGHTING, AND NOW HE'S DYING. BUT HOW? HE'S BEEN LOCKED IN HIS CELL ALONE.

48

TELL US, MR. RENFIELD.

I AM DYING! I HAVE BUT A FEW MINUTES.

HE BECKONED ME TO THE WINDOW.

EVERY ONE A LIFE! ALL RED BLOOD!

SEWARD CALLS FOR VAN HELSING. RENFIELD MUST STAY ALIVE LONG ENOUGH TO EXPLAIN!

HE SAYS HE SAW DRACULA SEVERAL TIMES, RIGHT OUTSIDE THE HOSPITAL.

DRACULA OFFERED RENFIELD MILLIONS OF RATS AND FLIES. IN RETURN, RENFIELD PROMISED OBEDIENCE—AND INVITED DRACULA INTO THE HOSPITAL.[1]

HE HAD BEEN TAKING THE LIFE OUT OF HER!

HE RAISED ME UP AND FLUNG ME DOWN.

TONIGHT, DRACULA APPEARED AGAIN, AND RENFIELD ATTACKED HIM. HE REALIZED THAT DRACULA HAD BEEN TRYING TO PREY ON MINA AND WANTED TO STOP HIM. BUT VAMPIRES HAVE SUPERHUMAN STRENGTH, AND RENFIELD WAS FATALLY WOUNDED.

1. INVITED DRACULA INTO THE HOSPITAL: ACCORDING TO LEGEND, VAMPIRES CANNOT ENTER A PLACE FOR THE FIRST TIME UNLESS THEY ARE INVITED BY SOMEONE INSIDE.

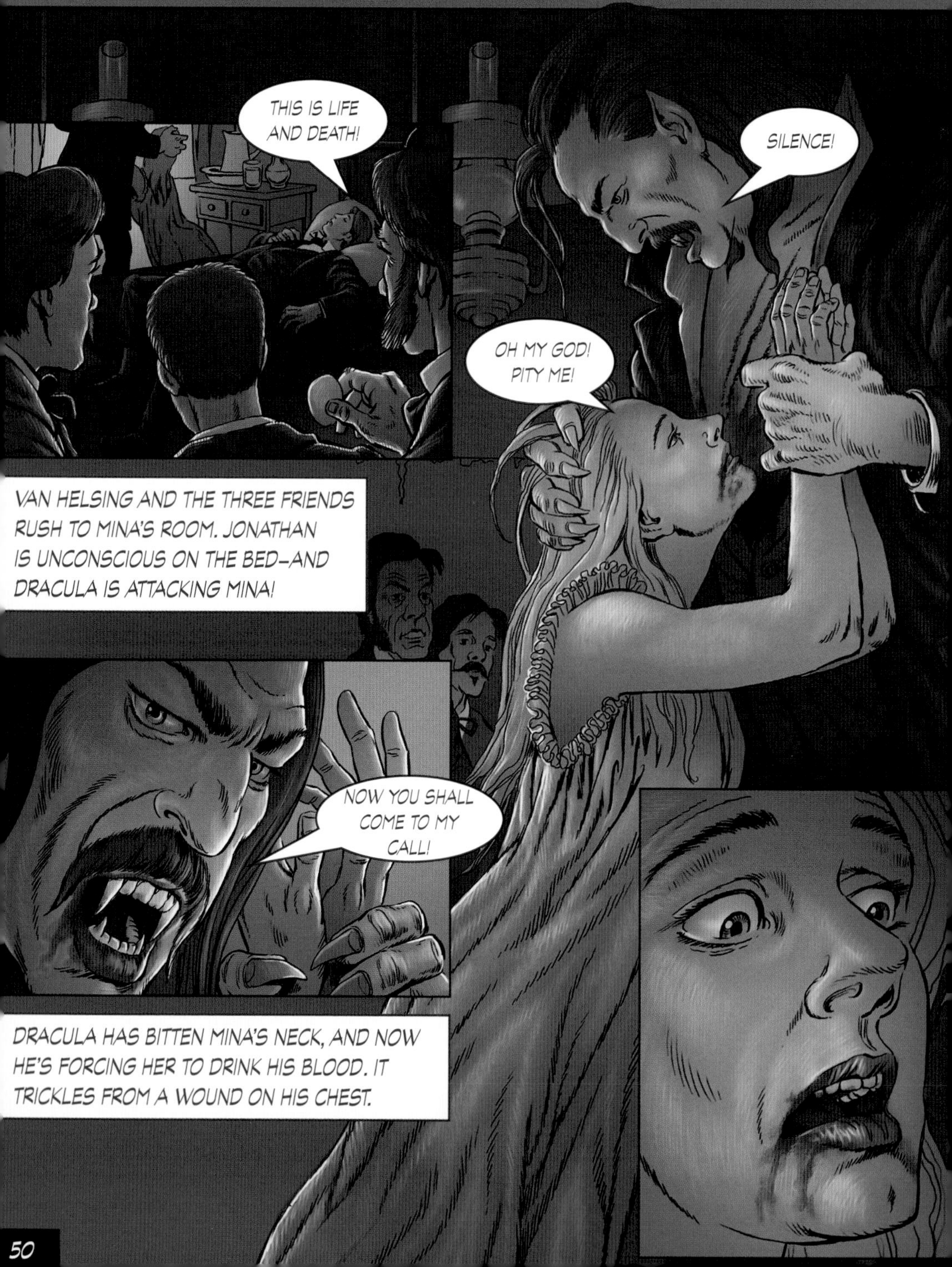

THIS IS LIFE AND DEATH!
SILENCE!
OH MY GOD! PITY ME!
VAN HELSING AND THE THREE FRIENDS RUSH TO MINA'S ROOM. JONATHAN IS UNCONSCIOUS ON THE BED—AND DRACULA IS ATTACKING MINA!
NOW YOU SHALL COME TO MY CALL!
DRACULA HAS BITTEN MINA'S NECK, AND NOW HE'S FORCING HER TO DRINK HIS BLOOD. IT TRICKLES FROM A WOUND ON HIS CHEST.

VAN HELSING SPRINGS TOWARD HIM WITH A CRUCIFIX AND WAFER. DRACULA IS MAD WITH RAGE BUT IS FORCED TO RETREAT, GROWLING AND SNARLING.

QUINCEY MORRIS AND ARTHUR CHASE AFTER DRACULA. VAN HELSING TRIES TO WAKE JONATHAN.

WHAT HAVE I DONE TO DESERVE SUCH A FATE?

MINA IS HYSTERICAL, SCREAMING AND CRYING. SHE HAS BITE MARKS ON HER NECK, JUST LIKE LUCY'S.

"GOOD GOD, HELP US!"

DRACULA'S BLOOD HAS MADE MINA HIS SLAVE. HE NOW HAS THE POWER TO CONTROL HER MIND. BUT MINA SAYS SHE'D RATHER DIE.

"HELP HER! OH, HELP HER!"

VAN HELSING SAYS SHE MUST STAY ALIVE UNTIL THEY HAVE KILLED DRACULA. OTHERWISE, SHE HERSELF WILL TURN INTO A VAMPIRE . . .

. . . AND HAVE TO DRINK BLOOD, LIKE LUCY.

"WE HAVE THIS DAY TO HUNT OUT ALL HIS LAIRS."

BY NOW IT'S DAYLIGHT. VAN HELSING SAYS THEY MUST CATCH DRACULA BEFORE NIGHTFALL. THEY'LL PURIFY HIS BOXES, SO HE CAN'T USE THEM TO SLEEP IN–ALL EXCEPT ONE BOX, WHERE THEY'LL TRAP HIM AND KILL HIM.

IF GOD WILL LET ME LIVE, I SHALL STRIVE TO DO SO.

DO NOT FEAR, MY DEAR.

THE MEN MUST GO OUT TO HUNT DRACULA, BUT MINA MUST REST AT HOME. BRAVELY SHE SAYS THAT SHE WILL CONTINUE TO WORK—AND TRY TO GO ON LIVING.

MINA SHOULD BE SAFE. SURELY DRACULA WILL NOT DARE ATTACK AGAIN BEFORE NIGHTFALL?

AAARGH!

FOR EXTRA SAFETY, VAN HELSING BLESSES MINA WITH A HOLY WAFER. BUT IT BURNS HER FLESH AND LEAVES A SINISTER BLOOD-RED SCAR!

COULD SHE BE TURNING INTO A VAMPIRE ALREADY?

THE MEN HURRY TO CARFAX CHAPEL AND SCATTER HOLY WAFERS IN THE BOXES THERE. DRACULA CAN'T HIDE IN THEM ANYMORE—BUT HE STILL HAS HIS OTHER BOXES, ALL HIDDEN.

THEY TRACK DOWN MOST OF THEM IN DRACULA'S NEW LONDON HOUSE AND OTHER PLACES IN THE CITY.

BY THE END OF THE DAY THEY HAVE FOUND ALL EXCEPT ONE. DRACULA MUST HAVE HIDDEN IT KNOWING VAN HELSING WOULD BE LOOKING FOR IT!

THEY GO BACK TO WAIT IN DRACULA'S HOUSE. THEY PLAN TO ATTACK HIM AS HE WALKS IN.

AT LAST THEY HEAR DRACULA COMING! HIS KEY TURNS IN THE LOCK, AND HIS HEAVY FOOTSTEPS GET CLOSER. THE FRIENDS ARE TENSE AND EAGER, READY TO LEAP OUT AT HIM.

1. ARMS: WEAPONS; ALSO THINGS FOR THEIR PROTECTION, SUCH AS CRUCIFIXES AND GARLIC.

GRRRRR!

DRACULA IS FAR TOO QUICK AND STRONG FOR THEM. HE SMASHES THE KNIVES FROM THEIR HANDS.

YOU SHALL BE SORRY YET!

THE FRIENDS TRY TO FORCE HIM INTO A CORNER. DRACULA BACKS AWAY FROM THEIR CRUCIFIXES ...

...THEN HURLS HIMSELF FORWARD AND KNOCKS THEM TO THE FLOOR. HE RUSHES ACROSS THE ROOM AND LEAPS THROUGH THE WINDOW.

CRASH!

MY REVENGE HAS JUST BEGUN! TIME IS ON MY SIDE!

WE HAVE LEARNED SOMETHING: HE FEARS US!

WITH A SCORNFUL LOOK, DRACULA RUNS AWAY, DROPPING SOME OF THE MONEY HE'S SAVED FOR HIS ESCAPE. AGAIN HE'S GOTTEN AWAY FROM THEM!

THE FRIENDS ARE DOWNHEARTED. BUT VAN HELSING TELLS THEM NOT TO WORRY; DRACULA HAS LEFT MANY CLUES BEHIND.

I KNOW THAT YOU MUST FIGHT, BUT . . .

. . . YOU MUST BE PITIFUL TO HIM, TOO!

THEY HURRY BACK TO DR. SEWARD'S HOSPITAL, WHERE MINA IS WAITING FOR THEM. THEY FIND SHE HAS AN UNEXPECTED FAVOR TO ASK THEM.

MINA BEGS THEM TO HELP DRACULA'S SOUL FIND PEACE, JUST AS THEY HELPED HER POOR FRIEND LUCY. THE MEN ALL WEEP. MINA IS SO KIND AND FORGIVING!

I HAVE AN IDEA.

DARKNESS . . .
SAILORS SHOUTING . . .

BEFORE THEY CAN KILL DRACULA,
VAN HELSING AND HIS FRIENDS
MUST TRACK HIM DOWN. MINA
THINKS SHE MAY BE ABLE TO
DISCOVER WHERE HE IS HIDING.

EVER SINCE MINA DRANK DRACULA'S BLOOD, HE CAN
"SPEAK" TO HER JUST BY THINKING. SHE ASKS VAN HELSING
TO HYPNOTIZE HER–HE MAY BE ABLE TO FIND OUT WHAT
DRACULA IS THINKING.

HAVE I BEEN
TALKING IN MY
SLEEP?

WE MUST
FIND HIM!

DRACULA MUST BE
ON BOARD A SHIP.
MINA IS DELIGHTED;
SURELY SHE'LL
BE SAFE NOW IF
DRACULA HAS
LEFT ENGLAND?

NO! GRIMLY, VAN HELSING
EXPLAINS THAT MINA'S STILL IN
DANGER. UNLESS THEY CAN KILL
DRACULA WHILE SHE IS STILL
ALIVE, SHE'LL STAY A VAMPIRE.

HEARING THIS DREADFUL NEWS,
MINA FAINTS.

HE IS CLEVER, OH SO CLEVER!

...WITH EYES THAT SEEMED TO BE BURNING...

THE FRIENDS FIND WHICH SHIPS HAVE JUST SAILED TOWARD TRANSYLVANIA. NEWSPAPERS REPORT THAT THERE'S ONLY ONE— THE *CZARINA' CATHERINE.*

AS FAST AS THEY CAN, THEY HURRY TO THE LONDON DOCKS. A DOCK WORKER TELLS THEM THAT A TALL, PALE MAN BOARDED THE *CATHERINE*—TAKING A BIG, HEAVY BOX AS CARGO.

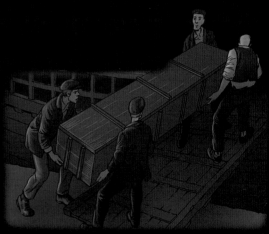

THEY ALSO HEAR THAT THE *CATHERINE* WAS LATE LEAVING PORT BECAUSE A MYSTERIOUS FOG DELAYED IT. THE FOG APPEARED WHEN THE CAPTAIN ARGUED WITH THE TALL, PALE MAN...

...BUT THE FOG AND THE MAN VANISHED WHEN THE BIG BOX WAS LOADED. THE DOCK WORKERS DON'T KNOW WHY, BUT VAN HELSING UNDERSTANDS; DRACULA IS ON BOARD THE SHIP, HIDING IN HIS LAST BOX OF DIRT.

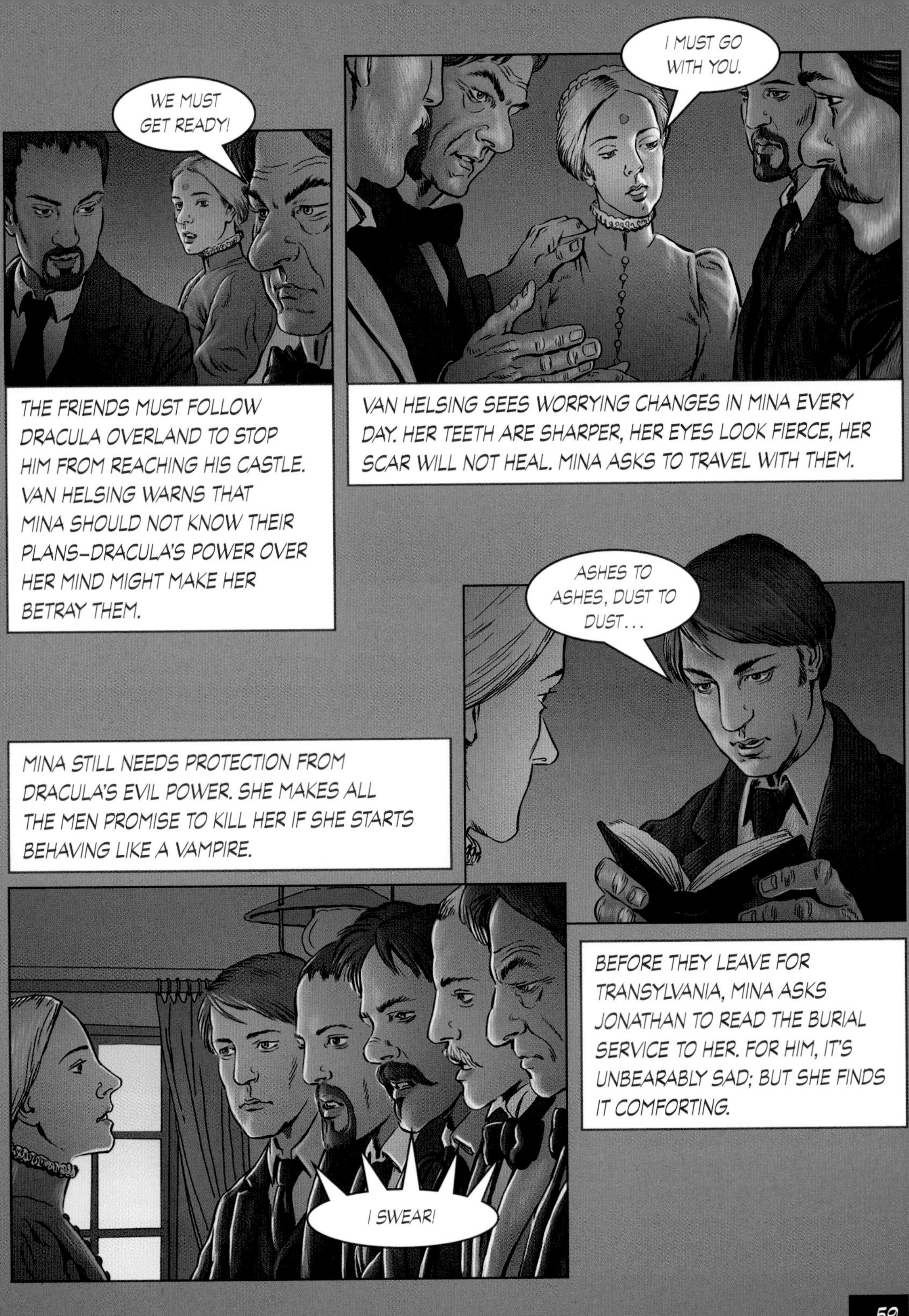
WE MUST GET READY!
THE FRIENDS MUST FOLLOW DRACULA OVERLAND TO STOP HIM FROM REACHING HIS CASTLE. VAN HELSING WARNS THAT MINA SHOULD NOT KNOW THEIR PLANS—DRACULA'S POWER OVER HER MIND MIGHT MAKE HER BETRAY THEM.
I MUST GO WITH YOU.
VAN HELSING SEES WORRYING CHANGES IN MINA EVERY DAY. HER TEETH ARE SHARPER, HER EYES LOOK FIERCE, HER SCAR WILL NOT HEAL. MINA ASKS TO TRAVEL WITH THEM.
ASHES TO ASHES, DUST TO DUST . . .
MINA STILL NEEDS PROTECTION FROM DRACULA'S EVIL POWER. SHE MAKES ALL THE MEN PROMISE TO KILL HER IF SHE STARTS BEHAVING LIKE A VAMPIRE.
BEFORE THEY LEAVE FOR TRANSYLVANIA, MINA ASKS JONATHAN TO READ THE BURIAL SERVICE TO HER. FOR HIM, IT'S UNBEARABLY SAD; BUT SHE FINDS IT COMFORTING.
I SWEAR!

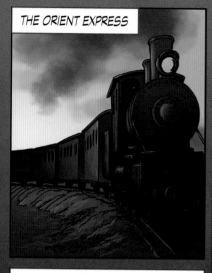

THE ORIENT EXPRESS

THEY ALL CATCH THE FAST TRAIN TO VARNA, THE RUSSIAN PORT ON THE BLACK SEA TO WHICH DRACULA'S SHIP IS HEADING.

THE MEN PREPARE DEADLY WEAPONS—GUNS AND SHARP KNIVES. MINA'S MOOD KEEPS CHANGING: SOMETIMES SHE'S RESTLESS AND ALERT, SOMETIMES DULL AND SLEEPY.

BRILLIANT!

DRACULA REALIZES HE'S BEING CHASED AND CUTS HIS MIND OFF FROM MINA. BUT SHE'S STILL ABLE TO WORK OUT THAT HE'S FOLLOWING AN

FOLLOW HIM!

THE FRIENDS LEAVE THE TRAIN AND SPLIT INTO THREE GROUPS. JONATHAN AND ARTHUR TAKE A STEAMBOAT ON THE RIVER.

SEWARD AND QUINCEY MORRIS
RIDE ON HORSEBACK OVER WILD MOUNTAINS.

FOLLOW!

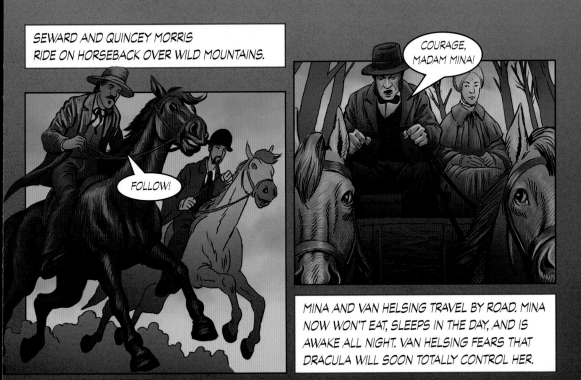

COURAGE,
MADAM MINA!

MINA AND VAN HELSING TRAVEL BY ROAD. MINA
NOW WON'T EAT, SLEEPS IN THE DAY, AND IS
AWAKE ALL NIGHT. VAN HELSING FEARS THAT
DRACULA WILL SOON TOTALLY CONTROL HER.

NOVEMBER 4, 1897

HERE YOU
ARE SAFE!

THEY CAMP NEAR DRACULA'S CASTLE.
VAN HELSING SURROUNDS MINA WITH
A CIRCLE OF HOLY WAFERS. SHE NEEDS
SPECIAL PROTECTION AGAINST THE CASTLE'S
DEADLY MAGIC.

COME
TO US!

COME, SISTER!

COME!

THAT NIGHT, MINA IS VISITED BY THE CASTLE'S
BEAUTIFUL, BLOOD-SUCKING WOMEN. THEY
CALL HER TO JOIN THEM. MINA IS PARALYZED
WITH HORROR.

NOVEMBER 5, 1897

I WILL GO TO MY TERRIBLE WORK.

I HEAR THE HOWL OF WOLVES.

LEAVING MINA SAFE INSIDE THE CIRCLE, VAN HELSING BRAVELY ENTERS DRACULA'S CASTLE.

HE IS LOOKING FOR THE CHAPEL AND THE TOMBS WHERE THE THREE BEAUTIFUL WOMEN SLEEP DURING THE DAY.

MEANWHILE . . .

HE HAMMERS A STAKE THROUGH EACH WOMAN'S VAMPIRE HEART AND CUTS OFF THEIR HEADS. THEIR BODIES GROW OLD AND WITHER.

DRACULA'S BOX ARRIVES IN A ROMA WAGON. THE FOUR FRIENDS COME GALLOPING AFTER IT. THEY FIGHT, AND QUINCEY IS BADLY WOUNDED.

DRACULA'S BOX
CRASHES OUT OF THE
WAGON.

LOOK! THE CURSE
HAS PASSED AWAY!

THEY KILL HIM BEFORE HE CAN STIR. DRACULA'S
EVIL POWER HAS ENDED. AS HE DIES, MINA
SEES A LOOK OF PEACE ON HIS FACE AT LAST—
BEFORE HE CRUMBLES AWAY TO DUST.

BRAVE QUINCEY MORRIS DIES FROM HIS
WOUNDS. BUT HE DIES HAPPY BECAUSE THE
SCAR ON MINA'S FOREHEAD HAS FINALLY
VANISHED. SHE'S HUMAN AGAIN! SHE'S SAVED!

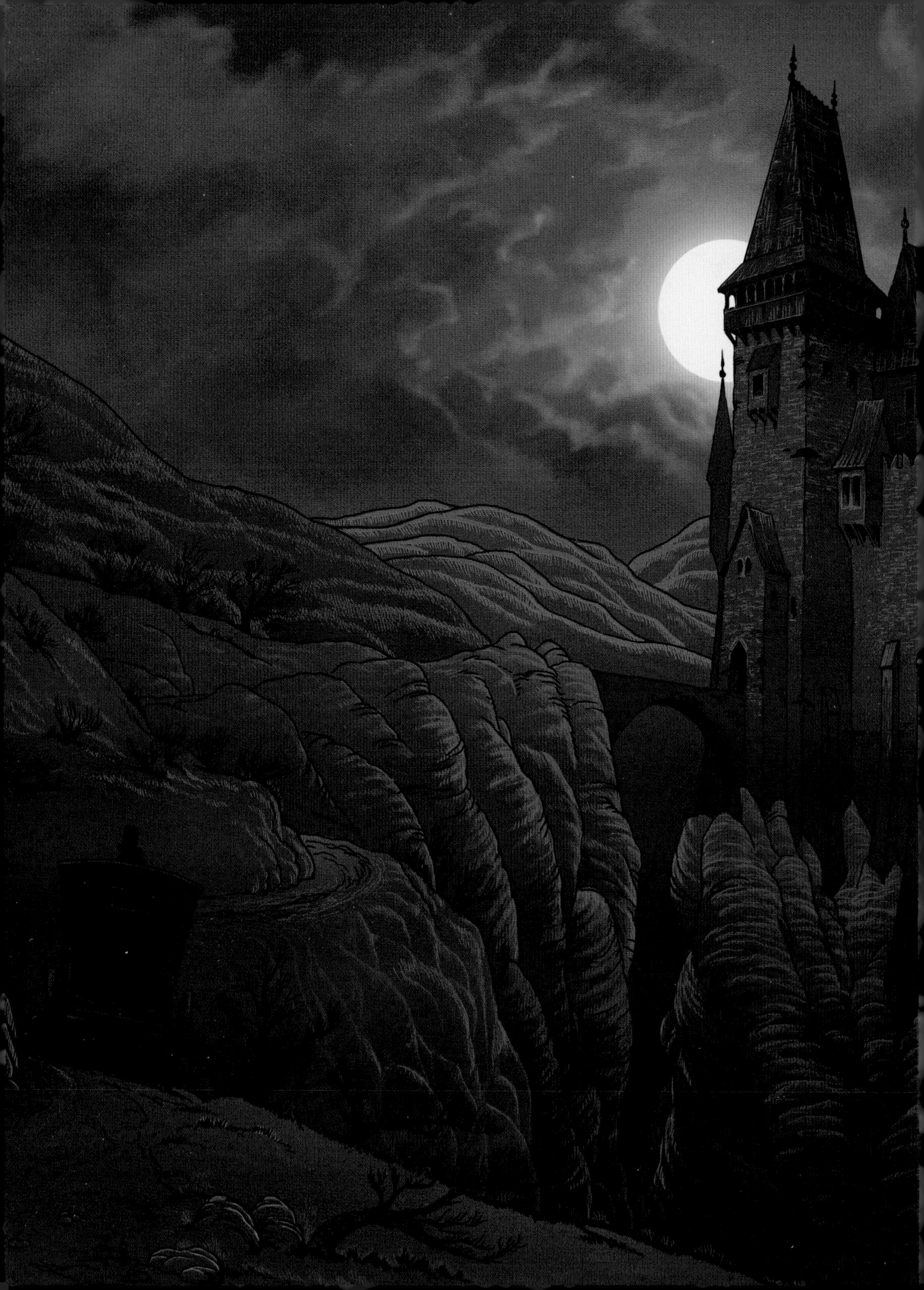